Fantastic Fairy Tales

SNOW WHITE AND THE SEVEN DWARFS

An imprint of Om Books International

One snowy winter morning, a queen sat sewing by her window. As she looked out at the beautiful palace gardens, she pricked her finger with the needle. She quickly put her finger in the snow collected around the ebony windowsill. The snow turned a rosy pink.

"Oh, how I wish I had a child as fair as the snow, with rosy lips and cheeks, and hair as black as ebony," thought the queen.

Time passed and the king and queen were blessed with a lovely baby girl, as beautiful as the queen had wished. They named her Snow White.

Alas, the queen died when Snow White was still a baby, and the king married again.

The new queen was an evil witch. She had made herself beautiful with magic. Every day, she would ask her magic mirror, "Mirror, mirror on the wall, who's the fairest of us all?"

And every day, the mirror would reply, "You are the most beautiful, my Queen."

Until one day, many years later, when Snow White had grown up into a lovely young girl, the mirror said to the queen, "O Queen, though a beauty you are, Snow White is more beautiful than you !"

The queen turned red with anger! "Snow White must die!" she told her huntsman. "Take her to the wild woods and bring me back her heart."

And so the huntsman took Snow White to the deep woods on his horse. At first he planned to kill her, but then he thought it would be a very cruel thing to do. So he let Snow White go away, warning her never to come back to the castle or the wicked queen would kill her.

Poor Snow White turned pale with fear in the dark woods. The night creatures made terrible sounds, scaring her a great deal.

“I wish someone would help me!” wailed Snow White, running helter-skelter. Just then, she spotted a little cottage.

Inside the cottage were seven little beds, seven little chairs at the table and a meal laid down for exactly seven people. Snow White was hungry and sleepy and the cottage looked warm and inviting. So she promptly ate from one plate and went off to sleep in a tiny little bed.

Now, the cottage belonged to seven dwarfs. And what a strange sight awaited them when they reached home! Finally, when Snow White woke up, she told them her sad story and the kind dwarfs agreed to let her stay with them.

The seven dwarfs were carpenters and would set out bright and early for their workshop deep in the woods. Snow White would look after the cottage - cleaning, cooking and sewing. She would sing to herself happily and was very content living with the kind dwarfs.

But alas! One day, the magic mirror told the evil queen that Snow White was still alive and was the most beautiful of all. So the wicked queen made a poisonous magic potion and coated some apples with it. She then disguised herself as a poor old fruit seller and left for the woods.

Finding Snow White at the cottage, she said, "Try these sugary sweet apples, my child. I have travelled far…Oh I am so tired, and I must sell these apples! Won't you just take a bite…"

The apples did look truly delicious and Snow White wanted to help the poor old lady too. And so she took a bite. The minute the juice of the apple touched her lips, the poison acted and Snow White fell down as if dead!

"Ha-ha-ha!" cackled the evil queen, and ran away saying, "I am the fairest one of all!"

That evening, the dwarfs came back with a beautiful bed they had made for Snow White to thank her for caring for them. They were very fond of their gentle friend and when they saw her lying as if dead on the ground, they burst into tears!

"Who could have done this to our dear girl?" they all cried.

Night and day, the dwarfs sat by Snow White, who slept on the bed they had made for her. One fine day, a handsome prince

came riding by and saw the lovely damsel asleep. He instantly fell in love with Snow White and kissed her. Lo and behold! Snow White woke up, as the poisonous apple fell from her mouth!

She thanked the prince for saving her and told him and the dwarfs what had happened. The prince locked away the evil queen in the dungeon, and she was never to be seen again!

Soon, the handsome prince and the lovely Snow White were married with much fanfare. The dwarfs too rejoiced with the entire kingdom, and they all lived happily ever after.